HOW PIZZA
CAME TO QUEENS

DAYAL KAUR KHALSA

CLARKSON N. POTTER, INC./PUBLISHERS
DISTRIBUTED BY CROWN PUBLISHERS, INC./NEW YORK

For
Guru Nanak,
Guru Amar Das,
and
Hari Amrit Kaur

ong ago, before there were pizza stands and pizzerias and frozen pizza and pizza mixes, there was hardly anything good to eat in May's town.

A hungry child asking for a snack might be handed a grape jelly sandwich or some cookies or a pretzel stick. There was no such thing as pizza.

But all that changed when Mrs. Pelligrino came to visit.

ay's best friends were three sisters, Linda, Judy, and Peggy Penny. She played with them all the time. One summer, when May's parents went away on vacation, she stayed at the Pennys' house.

One day Mrs. Penny told May that a distant cousin, whom she had never met, was coming from Italy for a visit. She said she thought Mrs. Pelligrino didn't speak much English.

rs. Pelligrino arrived in a taxi. She was clutching a strangely shaped green package very tightly to her chest. May and Linda thought it was a present. But when they reached to take it from her, Mrs. Pelligrino drew back sharply and snapped, "You no touch!"

She marched into the house and went straight into the kitchen. She sniffed in long and deep several times in every direction. Then she frowned and muttered, "Is no good."

Did the house smell bad? May and Linda and Judy and Peggy all sniffed in deeply, but the kitchen smelled all right to them.

he might just need a little time to adjust to the change," Mrs. Penny told the girls. "Let's leave her alone for a while." She took Mrs. Pelligrino into the dining room and brought her a cup of tea.

May and Linda watched her from the kitchen doorway. May whispered in Linda's ear, "I don't think it was a real present anyway—the bows are too little." Actually, it looked like a big green towel all rolled up.

Even after she drank her tea, Mrs. Pelligrino still looked unhappy. Every once in a while she lifted her nose in the air and inhaled deeply. She patted her strange green package and sighed sadly. "No pizza."

Pizza?

May and Linda looked at each other and shrugged their shoulders. They had no idea what she meant. Neither did Mrs. Penny. None of them had ever heard the word *pizza* before. The only Italian words they knew were spaghetti, macaroni, and lasagna. They couldn't even ask Mrs. Pelligrino what was the matter. And Mrs. Pelligrino didn't speak enough English to tell them.

Mrs. Penny took Mrs. Pelligrino up to her room and tried to make her as comfortable as possible. Judy and Peggy carried her suitcases upstairs, but when May and Linda tried to carry her green package, once again Mrs. Pelligrino clasped it to her chest and warned, "No touch."

They didn't think they were going to enjoy Mrs. Pelligrino's visit very much.

When Mrs. Penny came back downstairs, she said, "I wonder who Pizza is? Mrs. Pelligrino seems to miss her very much. Maybe it's her daughter?"

"Or her dog?" said Judy.

"We could buy her one," suggested May.

"Maybe it's a kind of flower," said Linda.

But Peggy thought perhaps *pizza* was the name of the town in Italy where she lived.

"Well, whatever or whoever *pizza* is," said Mrs. Penny, "Mrs. Pelligrino is our guest and we must all try to make her visit as happy as we can."

t wasn't easy.

The girls put on a special play with a very happy ending to try to cheer her up. And while Mrs. Pelligrino seemed to enjoy it and clapped loudly, by suppertime she was her old sad self again.

They pooled all their allowances and took her out to eat at their favorite restaurant.

When she walked in, Mrs. Pelligrino sniffed in deeply and actually smiled. May and Linda and Judy and Peggy were so relieved. But when the waitress brought their grilled cheese sandwiches, Mrs. Pelligrino looked down at the little toasted squares and shook her head mournfully. "No pizza."

hey tried hard to think of new ways to make her happy.

    May and Linda even did what they did whenever they had a fight and were feeling bad afterwards. They took all their toys and put them together in one huge display in the yard. This always made them feel very happy. But while Mrs. Pelligrino looked carefully at every toy, saying "Nice, nice," they could tell she still wasn't really happy deep inside.

rs. Pelligrino was also trying hard to be happy. She took part in all their games.

Whenever Mrs. Penny went shopping, she let May and Linda take the groceries into their play store. Then she would come with pennies and buy back everything she needed to make supper. Mrs. Pelligrino liked this game a lot.

 n the evenings she brought them milk and pretzels and watched them chase fireflies.

ut the only time Mrs. Pelligrino seemed to really cheer up was when she was cooking. Somehow the gentle bubbling of tomato sauce soothed her spirits. Fortunately they all loved spaghetti. "I could eat spaghetti even for breakfast," said May.

Despite everyone's best efforts, still Mrs. Pelligrino would sniff in deeply now and then—and the old sadness would be upon her again.

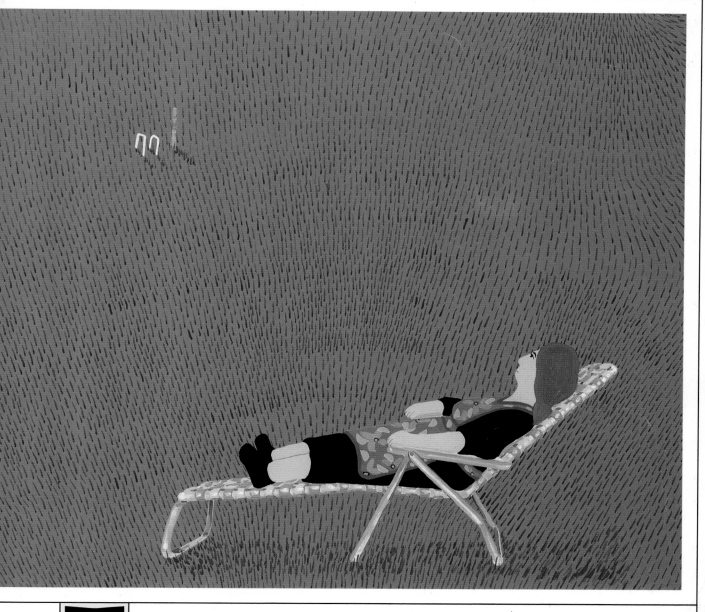

The girls had grown very fond of Mrs. Pelligrino. They wanted to make her really happy at least once before she had to leave. The key seemed to be connected to the word *pizza*. If only they could find out what it meant. May had an idea where they could try.

They went to the library. The librarian helped them look it up in the dictionary: *piz-za* (pēt′ sa) *n:* an Italian baked dish consisting of a shallow pie-like crust covered usually with a spiced mixture of tomatoes and cheese.

"Pie-like? With tomatoes?" said Peggy.

 udy suggested they look in a cookbook.

They had to look in a lot of cookbooks before they finally found one with a recipe for *Pizza Pie*. Peggy copied out the list of ingredients: yeast, flour, tomato paste, mozzarella cheese, parmesan cheese, olive oil, garlic, oregano, and pepper.

"It sure doesn't sound like pie to me," said May.

"Yuk," said Linda. They all agreed it sounded terrible. But—if it would make Mrs. Pelligrino happy—they would try anything.

he next day they went shopping and bought everything on the list.
Mrs. Pelligrino knocked on the wall of their play store. "What you got for me today?" she asked.

May and Linda began handing her the things they had bought. With each item her smile grew bigger. By the time they gave her the garlic, Mrs. Pelligrino was beaming. "Pizza!" she cried joyfully. She cradled the ingredients in her arms and hurried into the house. She looked very, very happy.

rs. Pelligrino brought her strangely shaped green package down to the kitchen and put it on the table. May and Linda still hoped it might be a present. She unwrapped it carefully. It was—a rolling pin! Mrs. Pelligrino smiled at it like an old friend. May and Linda frowned. "No be sad," said Mrs. Pelligrino. "We make pizza."

She showed them how to make dough and then roll it out into a circle with the rolling pin. Then she taught them how to throw the dough high in the air to stretch it. She spread tomato sauce on each big circle and the girls sprinkled them with cheese.

s the pizza baked and the cheese began to bubble, the whole house was filled with the most wonderful smell they had ever smelled. It smelled as good as toast and french fries and ketchup and grilled cheese sandwiches and spaghetti all rolled into one. They sniffed in long and deep.

Mrs. Penny came into the kitchen. "What is that delicious smell?" she asked.

"It's pizza!" they cried.

hen the pizza was done, they had a party. May called her grandma to come over, and the mailman, who happened to be delivering the mail just then, joined in. Everyone thought pizza was the best thing they ever tasted.

Mrs. Pelligrino was very happy. "Ah, pizza! Is good, no?" she said proudly.

"Yes!" they all yelled.

And that's how pizza came to Queens.

 fter that, Mrs. Pelligrino was happy all the time. She made pizza every day. Everyone said Mrs. Pelligrino was the best guest they had ever met. The whole neighborhood smelled wonderful.

he time soon came for Mrs. Pelligrino to go home to Italy.

On her last day, May and Linda and Judy and Peggy decided it was their turn to cook for Mrs. Pelligrino.

They made her toast and jelly and served her breakfast in bed.

veryone was sad to see Mrs. Pelligrino go. They made her promise to come back again next year.

"And meanwhile," said May, "every time we have pizza, we'll think of you."

Published by Clarkson N. Potter, Inc., 225 Park Avenue South, New York, New York 10003 and represented in Canada by the Canadian MANDA Group.

CLARKSON N. POTTER, POTTER, and colophon are trademarks of Clarkson N. Potter, Inc.

Manufactured in Japan

Library of Congress Cataloging-in-Publication Data

Khalsa, Dayal Kaur.
How pizza came to Queens / story and pictures by Dayal Kaur
Khalsa.
p.   cm.
Summary: An Italian visitor to Queens bemoans the unavailability
of pizza until some thoughtful girls enable her to make some.
[1. Pizza—Fiction.   2. Queens (New York, N.Y.)—Fiction.]
I. Title.
PZ7.K52647Ho   1989   88-22452
[Fic]—dc19   CIP

ISBN 0-517-57126-9

10 9 8 7 6 5 4 3 2 1

First Edition